Mr. Dickens Hits Town

TUNDRA BOOKS

Mr. Dickens Hits Town

Text by Jan Mark

Illustrated by Regolo Ricci

Published in Canada by Tundra Books, *McClelland & Stewart Young Readers*,
481 University Avenue, Toronto, Ontario M5G 2E9

Published in the United States by Tundra Books of Northern New York,
P.O. Box 1030, Plattsburgh, New York 12901

Library of Congress Catalog Number: 99-70965

Canadian Cataloguing in Publication Data

Mark, Jan
Mr. Dickens hits town

ISBN 0-88776-468-1

I. Dickens, Charles, 1812-1870 – Journeys – Quebec(Province) – Montréal – Juvenile fiction. I. Ricci, Regolo. II. Title.

PZ7.M33924Mr 1999 j823'.914 C99-930626-X

We acknowledge the support of the Canada Council for the Arts and the Ontario Arts Council for our publishing program.

We acknowledge the financial support of the Government of Canada through the Book Publishing Industry Development Program for our publishing activities.

Canadä

Printed and bound in Spain
D.L. TO: 1218- 1999

1 2 3 4 5 6 04 03 02 01 00 99

For Janet Lunn

J.M.

For Gail and for Enzo

R.R.

NICHOLAS
NICKLEBY
DICKENS

CAST OF CHARACTERS

These people were real:

Mr. Charles Dickens
Mrs. Kate Dickens
Mrs. Perry
Earl of Mulgrave
Mrs. Torrens
Captain Torrens
Captain Willoughby
Captain Granville
Lieutenant Tom Methuen
Dr. Griffen
Mr. Ermatinger
Mrs. Ermatinger
Miss Jane Ermatinger

And these people might have been:

Major Perry
Mary Perry
Dorothy Perry
William Perry
Grandmother Perry
Lieutenant Hugh Lincoln
M. Arnoux
Mme Arnoux
Henriette Arnoux
Mlle Fleurie
M. Hardouin
Amalie
Private Page
Mrs. Darcy
The parrot

"BRITANNIA"

In 1842 the great English novelist Charles Dickens made his famous tour of America. His visit to Montreal, on the way home, is less famous.

Invited to look in on the Garrison Players by the Earl of Mulgrave, a stagestruck young officer, the equally stagestruck Dickens planned the program and took the leading roles, acting as director and stage manager at the same time.

It must have been a memorable experience for all concerned. This is what might have happened. Quite a lot of it is true. . . .

In which Dorothy Perry visits the neighbors and Lieutenant Lincoln brings exciting news:

At Christmas Grandmother Perry writes from England and presses flowers between the pages of her letter. In January, when the mails arrive (delayed by Atlantic gales and run aground off Halifax), Dorothy takes the flowers to show Henriette Arnoux, who lives next door to the house rented by Dorothy's father.

"This is an aconite," Dorothy explains, displaying the frail petals on the end of their brittle stem, "and this is winter heliotrope, Mama says." The winter heliotrope smells very faintly of spring. "Only think, flowers growing in winter."

"We have flowers in the conservatory," Henriette says. Mme Arnoux had lilies on her table at Christmas. *Chez* Arnoux is far larger than the Perrys' house, for Monsieur Arnoux is a magistrate and

wealthy, but Papa is *Major* Perry. This counts for a good deal in society here. Dorothy is not envious.

"But these flowers grew out-of-doors. Grandmother picked them in the snow." She knows, and Henriette knows, that only by a miracle will they ever find flowers growing in December among the snows of Montreal.

Dorothy tucks the flowers back between the pages of her diary, where Mama has let her keep them for safety, and goes home again, along the white path between the houses, stomped out only this morning by Private Page, in his snowshoes.

While she has been visiting Henriette, Lieutenant Hugh Lincoln has arrived to see her sister, Mary, and is delivering his news at the top of his voice in the drawing room.

"Lord Mulgrave is back; that's what I came to tell you," Hugh is shouting. Why should he come all the way from the Quebec Gate Barracks to tell them that? The Earl of Mulgrave is *aide de camp* to the commander in chief, an amiable young man and a fine rider, but not so very exciting. "But," cries Lieutenant Lincoln, "he came over from Liverpool in the steam packet *Britannia* with Charles Dickens!"

In which Lieutenant Lincoln shares his exciting news and Mary Perry declines to be excited:

"Pray sit down, Mr. Lincoln," Mary says, crushingly. Dorothy is not deceived. Mary adores Charles Dickens, all the Perrys do. He is their favorite author; he is everyone's favorite author. Each installment of his latest book is awaited like news from the battlefield as it crosses the ocean and journeys up the St. Lawrence. Can he really have followed his books?

"He's here, in Canada?" William asks. William is the youngest Perry and, unlike Mary and Dorothy, has never seen England. The girls have visited Grandmother, and call England "home" as Papa does. To William, England is abroad.

"No, he's touring America – " Hugh twirls around and steps on Mary's skirt.

"*Do* sit down, Mr. Lincoln," Mary hisses.

"– and when he is done in America, he is crossing over. He is coming to Montreal in May, and Lord Mulgrave has invited him to direct our theatricals!"

"Is that all?" Mary lifts her embroidery tambour as if to hide a yawn, but Dorothy knows that she can scarcely speak for excitement. To save her the bother she says,

"And he's coming here? Charles Dickens is coming here? Shall we see him?"

"I'm sure Mr. Lincoln will see him," Mary says, recovering her

poise. "For if there are to be theatricals, Mr. Lincoln is sure to be in them." Mary has put away childish things. Each time a new play is performed, she makes it known that acting is very childish indeed. Not that this stops her from going to watch, at the Artillery Theatre in the barracks and at the Theatre Royal, for the really splendid productions. The army has its own company of actors, the Garrison Amateurs. Hugh Lincoln is one of them.

"Will you stay for tea, Hugh?" Mama asks, looking in from the hall. Mama treats Hugh as if he were already one of the family. Dorothy and William hope very much that Mary will unbend enough to make him one of the family, if he ever plucks up courage to propose. Lieutenant Lincoln has faced rebels and rioters in his time; like the rest of the garrison, he is here to protect the border – he would protect it with his life – but he is no match for Mary. Papa says he is all very well in his way, no harm in the boy, but what sort of a soldier is he going to make if he spends all his time fooling around at the playhouse?

Hugh is already gathering up his hat and gloves. "Thanks, but I won't stay. Have to leave straightaway. . . ."

"On duty?"

"Meeting of the Driving Club," Hugh says, cheerfully. "For the parade on Saturday, you know."

"Of course," Mary drawls. "It will be the most exciting thing to happen since the Patriote Rebellion."

This is not kind and not true, but it does seem that nothing entertaining ever happens in Montreal unless the military have a hand in it. It is the Driving Club that is putting on Saturday's parade of sleighs along Notre-Dame, and if it were not for the Garrison Amateurs, Charles Dickens would never think of coming to Montreal; and there are three wintry months to endure before that happens.

In which Mary is excited after all and her father is not:

Once Hugh is out of the door, Mary appears in the hall; all signs of boredom have vanished. "Mama?"

"Yes, dear?"

"Did you hear what Lieutenant Lincoln said about Charles Dickens coming here in May?"

"I should think they heard it down on Water Street," Mrs. Perry remarks.

"It would be too dreadful if Mr. Dickens came here and we did not meet him."

"I don't think we are likely to meet him," Mrs. Perry says. "But I dare say we might go to the play and *see* him."

"Oh, *Mama.*" Mary comes up very close and puts an arm around her mother. "I think it would be a very good idea if you were to join the Private Theatricals Committee."

"Which Private Theatricals Committee would that be?"

Mary has spent enough time listening to Hugh Lincoln to know exactly how these things are managed. "Oh, there has to be a committee to decide on the plays and the costumes, you know. Lord Mulgrave is always on it, and Mrs. Torrens said she would be, next time. There have to be ladies on the committee because of ladies acting in the plays."

"*You* are not thinking of acting, I hope," Major Perry says to his wife, when he comes home and hears the news.

C. DICKENS
WELL

"Perhaps a small role," says Mrs. Perry, "to keep Agnes Torrens company. But Mary and Hugh are very anxious that I should join the committee – Hugh because he thinks I would enjoy it, and Mary because she thinks that if I do, she might actually get a chance to meet Mr. Dickens."

"Why would she want to do that?" Major Perry knows perfectly well why. He admires Charles Dickens's novels as much as anyone, but he does not see the need to *meet* the fellow. He may turn out to be a bore – or worse.

Dorothy writes in her diary: *31 January 1842. Charles Dickens is coming to Montreal!*

In which the Private Theatricals Committee reads some plays, and then some more plays. Lord Mulgrave and Mr. Dickens write letters:

Dorothy discovers rapidly that Hugh has been quite wrong in thinking that Mama will enjoy being on the committee with Captain and Mrs. Torrens, Lord Mulgrave, and Mr. Ermatinger of the police force.

"I ought to enjoy it," Mama confesses, after two or three weeks. "I *would* enjoy it, were it not for Mr. Dickens."

"But he isn't here yet!" Mary protests. "He's still in New York."

"He might be on the moon for all the difference it would make," Mrs. Perry says. "We have had four meetings and read I don't know how many plays. Agnes wanted to do *The School for Scandal* and we thought that would go over very well, so Lord Mulgrave wrote to Mr. Dickens, but Mr. Dickens didn't reply, so we assumed he disagreed. And we went away and read another five dozen plays, and Captain Torrens suggested *A Roland for an Oliver,* which is very popular in England, apparently, and Mr. Ermatinger said his favorite was *The Young Widow,* so Lord Mulgrave wrote again to Mr. Dickens and he wrote back and said he didn't care for *The Young Widow* and what about *Deaf as a Post?*"

"A Roland for an Oliver"! says Hugh. "Why, that's a capital farce; I saw it done in London – at home, I mean. You have this old gentleman, Sir Mark Chase, who lives next door to a lunatic asylum –"

"I observe that there is always a deal of fun to be had at the expense of the insane," Major Perry remarks.

"Oh, there are no lunatics onstage," Hugh says, "but Sir Mark has promised to leave all his money to Mr. Selbourne if he marries Miss Darlington – Mr. Selbourne, that is – only he's already married, so he pretends his wife *isn't* his wife, and then he tells Alfred Highflyer that Sir Mark's house is the asylum – I forget why – and when Highflyer finds out Sir Mark isn't mad after all, he pretends *he's* mad, that is –"

"So," says Major Perry, "you propose to begin with a play in which a man pretends to be mad, and to finish with a play in which a man pretends to be deaf. What about the interlude – a man pretending to be dead, perhaps? Antoinette, my dear," he says to his wife, "perhaps you can persuade the committee to arrange for the audience to spend an evening in the graveyard. It would save us all a great deal of trouble and would be quite as entertaining."

"Wouldn't it be capital if we could put on *Nicholas Nickleby*?" Hugh says. "Why, when Charles Dickens was writing it, productions were appearing on the London stage."

"That must have been a singular undertaking," Major Perry says. "What happened at the final curtain each night? Did the manager step forward and ask the audience to come back in a month to see how the thing turned out?"

"Well, yes – no – I don't know," Hugh says. "But it would be splendid to produce Charles Dickens's own work, directed by Charles Dickens himself."

"I suppose we might suggest that," says Mrs. Perry, but the next morning Lord Mulgrave receives another letter, from Kingston. Mr. Dickens is only one day away and appears to have made up his own mind about the program: *A Roland for an Oliver; Past Two o'Clock in the Morning;* and *Deaf as a Post.*

"Then why did you read all those plays, Mama?" Dorothy asks.

"That is what committees are for," Mrs. Perry replies. "Passing time in doing something quite pointless that might otherwise be frittered away in useful work."

In which Lieutenant Lincoln arranges a treat and Mary has to miss it:

Dorothy and William corner Hugh Lincoln as he is leaving the house after one of his hopeful, but fruitless, visits to Mary.

"Has she said yes yet?" William says.

"I've not dared to ask her yet."

"I think," says Dorothy, "that if you could introduce us to Mr. Dickens, she will vow to be yours till death."

"I don't know about introducing you," says Hugh, "but I think I might arrange for you to get a look at him – and Mary, too, if she would care to come with us. Lord Mulgrave was going to meet him at Lachine, but he's got himself becalmed in his yacht in the middle of the St. Lawrence, so the commander in chief is sending his own four-in-hand to fetch him back to town. Now, I happen to know that he is putting up at Rasco's Hotel on St. Paul Street, because Tom Methuen has a room there. I dare say we could just happen to be passing at the right moment. Ask your mama if I may take you walking this afternoon. And ask Mary if she would like to join us."

But Mary has a lesson with her drawing master that afternoon, and Mama refuses to let her break the appointment. "I will *not* allow you to tell M. Hardouin that you have a cold and then have the whole town reporting that you were well enough to stand around in the wind on St. Paul Street. Mr. Dickens has been hounded by admirers all over America. I understand that he wishes to be private here."

However, she allows the children to go out with Lieutenant Lincoln and, after walking three times down St. Paul Street and twice up it, they see a four-in-hand approaching at the gallop from the western end. Dorothy and William immediately discover that their shoe buckles have come unfastened and stoop to adjust them, as they have been planning to do all along. By the sheerest luck they are exactly at the corner of Rasco's famous hotel, about to become more famous.

In which Mr. and Mrs. Dickens arrive in Montreal and Dorothy is not altogether impressed:

The coach pulls up. The door swings open, and out bounds a shortish young man with disordered wavy brown hair.

"Is that him?" William says. He has been expecting an elderly, white-headed giant with flowing whiskers.

"Must be," says Hugh, who has seen a picture of the great man.

Dorothy has imagined a slender, poetical person, and certainly something more dignified. Mr. Dickens has on a blue velvet coat, bottle-green trousers, embroidered shirt, and a canary-colored cravat, held in place with an amethyst pin. Growing up among soldiers, she and William are accustomed to the gorgeous colors of the military, but that does not prepare them for Mr. Dickens's vest, which is loud with red, purple, and gold stripes.

William nudges her. "I say, Dolly, isn't he *bright*?"

Mr. Dickens bounces on the balls of his feet and gulps lungsful of good dockside air. Behind him a little plump lady climbs out of the carriage, turns her foot on the step, and falls full length upon the sidewalk. Mr. Dickens and several gentlemen, including Lieutenant Lincoln, rush to assist her, while she laughs bravely and blushes and says that she is not hurt, no, not a bit.

"I declare, Kate, that is the seven hundred and forty-*fourth* time that you have fallen down since we left Liverpool," says Mr. Dickens, playfully. "Have you a limb or a digit left unbandaged?"

"Who is that poor lady?" William whispers loudly.

"I think that must be Mrs. Dickens," says Dorothy, as Hugh comes back to them.

"I didn't know he was married," William says, sounding faintly disapproving.

"My word, I'm fairly dazzled," says Hugh. "I think he must have a ring on every finger."

Dorothy is more than a little disappointed in Mr. Dickens. Mama would never fall down in the street in the way that Mrs. Dickens did, but if she had hurt herself, Papa would never laugh at her in the way that Mr. Dickens did.

In which Lieutenant Lincoln prepares to impress Mr. Dickens:

Here is Hugh again, hopeful in the hallway.

"No," says Mary, "I cannot possibly hear your lines, Mr. Lincoln. I am going to the soirée tonight with Mama and Papa."

"Well, so am I," Hugh says. "We all are, all the Garrison Amateurs. But if Mr. Dickens asks me if I know my part, I want to be able to say yes."

"I don't see why he'd bother to ask," says Mary, running upstairs. "If he is anything like you, he will only be worried about his own part."

"Oh, he's not going to act," Hugh says. "*He* will direct *us*."

"I'll hear your lines," Dorothy says, feeling sorry for Hugh. Mary was so nice to him yesterday, when she wanted to hear all about how Mr. Dickens arrived at Rasco's Hotel, and how he looked, and what he wore. Now that she is going to see him for herself, she has no time for poor Hugh, who follows Dorothy into the schoolroom like a sad dog that thought it was going to be taken ratting.

"Which is your part?" Dorothy asks, taking the little playbooks from Hugh.

"Well, Gallop in *Deaf as a Post,* but he's only a servant, a couple of lines," says Hugh. "But I'm playing Mr. Snobbington in *Past Two o'Clock.* That's a two-hander, just me and Captain Granville. Funniest thing out, don't you know, better than *A Roland for an Oliver.* I'm not in that, of course."

DOROTHY
PERRY

Hugh knows his part perfectly – a fussy old man who is woken up by a crazy stranger banging on his door in the middle of the night. Dorothy longs to see him onstage and says so, sending him away quite happy to dress for the soirée.

Not exactly everyone who is anyone in Montreal is going, but the party is being given by the Private Theatricals Committee and all the Garrison Amateurs will be there. Mama has sent invitations to M. and Mme Arnoux. Henriette knows little about Charles Dickens and cares less, but she knows about fame. Why should Dorothy Perry have all the glory?

"I am not allowed to read novels," she says piously. "Maman says they are scandalous."

"She's going to the soirée, though," Dorothy says.

In which Mr. Dickens begins to make his presence felt. Unfortunate incident with a wig:

At breakfast next morning William and Dorothy hear about the wonders of the night before.

"Did you really speak to him, Papa?" William asks. "Did you speak to Charles Dickens?"

"I did," Major Perry says, shortly. "I shook his hand, rings and all. Bells on his toes, I shouldn't wonder. I don't mind telling you that if I met him at home, I'm not at all sure that I'd have the fellow in the house. And whatever possessed you to invite him here –" He turns to his wife.

"He's coming *here*?" Dorothy squeaks.

"I told you, dearest, it was decided among the committee that there should be no public entertainments for Mr. and Mrs. Dickens; they had enough of that in America. We agreed to invite them to private dinners," Mama says.

"We didn't have to be the first, dammit," the major growls, and thunders away to go down to the barracks. William walks with him, as he always does when the weather is fine. Dorothy leans across the table to Mary and Mama.

"Was Mrs. Dickens there, too?"

"Of course she was." Mary is not interested in Mrs. Dickens.

"What did she wear?"

"Pink satin and court plasters," Mary says, waspishly.

"The poor girl is all over sprains and cuts and bruises," Mama says. "She even managed to fall downstairs –"

"Only the last three steps, Mama. And she landed on Captain Willoughby."

"It is three steps more than I should care to fall before the cream of Montreal society," Mrs. Perry says. "They must be quite tired of being stared at. It seems that they were treated like creatures in a menagerie in America; people lined up to stare through their stateroom window on the lake steamer."

"Did Hugh meet Mr. Dickens?" Dorothy asks and hopes that Mama will not notice that she has taken a second cup of coffee, which is forbidden.

"Oh, Mr. Lincoln is very much put out," says Mary, looking hard at Dorothy's guilty cup. "You know how he has been rattling on about Mr. Snobbington –"

"He has it perfect," Dorothy says loyally. "I heard his lines yesterday."

"Well, he has wasted his time. Mr. Dickens means to play Snobbington himself, *and* Gallop. He even ordered a special Snobbington wig from New York."

"I gather he did not imagine he could obtain such luxuries here," Mama says. "In fact I got the impression he thought we would be all be living in log cabins and grubbing up roots for dinner. Please don't think I am losing my eyesight, Dorothy: that cup was empty a moment ago. In any case, it is a hideous wig and he was running around with it, trying it on. Then Captain Granville made a very unfortunate remark about scalps, which offended the Ermatingers dreadfully."

"Why, Mama?"

"Charlotte Ermatinger was an Ojibway princess before she married. To speak of scalps was in the worst possible taste, and young Granville ought to have known better. I'm sure Charlotte never scalped anybody."

"Anyway," says Mary, "Mr. Lincoln is reduced to playing third gamekeeper, or tenth lunatic, or some such, after all his strutting about. And Mr. Methuen, who was to have played Alfred Highflyer, has been demoted to Sir Mark Chase, which is an inferior role, even if he is a baronet, and Mr. Dickens will play Highflyer too."

"As far as I can see," says Mrs. Perry, "they might just as well stay at home and let Mr. Dickens play all the parts himself."

Later, as she waits for William to come home so that they can join Mlle Fleurie in the schoolroom, Dorothy has an idea.

"Mama, I know that William and I may not stay up late for dinner, but won't you introduce us to Mr. Dickens when he arrives? Please, Mama? I think we're the only people in Montreal who haven't met him."

Mama gives her an odd, hard look, then smiles. "I shall certainly introduce you to *Mrs.* Dickens. She asked particularly to meet you. She is quite pining for her own little ones – four of them left at home, and all under five. I dare say Mr. Dickens may notice you."

In which Dorothy and William meet Mrs. Dickens, and Mr. Dickens meets Mary:

When Mrs. Dickens joins them next evening in a quiet corner of the drawing room, Dorothy sees what Mary meant about the court plasters. Mrs. Dickens wears one over her left eye, one on her right elbow, and two or three on the fingers of each hand.

"My poor babies," she sighs. "I have missed all their birthdays except Kate's second. Only think," she says to William, "how you would feel if you were not to see your own dear mama for six months. We shall not be home before the end of June as it is – if we ever reach home –"

"Why, don't lose heart now," says Mrs. Perry, alarmed at seeing Mrs. Dickens so upset. "I know the days must seem to get longer and longer –"

"Oh, it's not that," cries Mrs. Dickens, "but the voyage out, oh, such a storm, and the boat was a steamer – such a fear of fire when we were not in fear of drowning – I do pray that we may go home under sail – and the seasickness! I did not want to come at first, indeed I did not . . . but Mr. Dickens has been so very kind. . . ." Mrs. Dickens scrabbles for her handkerchief.

"I'm sure he has," says Mama. Dorothy thinks she has never seen her mother look so angry, but she takes Mrs. Dickens by the hand and smiles and says gently, "It was a winter crossing. You will be sure of a fair passage home, dear Kate."

Dorothy sees something bright, like a walking headache, crossing the room. It is Mr. Dickens himself, in cherry-colored plush with satin facings, royal-blue trousers, and a yellow vest. A pink geranium cringes in his buttonhole.

"Well, Kate, still in one piece? I see you have found some children to console you."

"My daughter Dorothy," says Mama. Dorothy bobs a curtsy. "My son William."

"Good evening, Miss Dorothy." He has the nicest smile. "Good evening to you, William."

William is blinking, dazzled. His mouth opens. He manages to reply.

"Sir; do you care for parrots?"

"There's no accounting for what children will say," Mrs. Dickens remarks, but Dorothy knows what William is thinking and so does Mama, she can tell.

"Parrots?" says Mr. Dickens. "Why, yes, William, exceedingly, though I do not have the good fortune to possess one. But at home I have an eagle and a very fine raven. I once had another raven, called Grip, now dead, alas. In fact," says Mr. Dickens, "my friends say that I am 'raven' mad."

Dorothy sees the joke before William does, and laughs. Mr. Dickens looks very much pleased, but then he seems to forget them both. Young ladies are entering the room – Miss Jane Ermatinger, followed by Mary. Mama rises.

"Mr. Dickens, Kate, I do not think you met my elder daughter the other evening. This is Mary."

Mary advances, smiling, and holds out her hand, but an awful change has come over Mr. Dickens. He turns pale.

"Mary?" he says. His voice has fallen a full octave. "There was another Mary . . ." Dorothy sees tears in his eyes. "Why, in Kingston it was the very anniversary . . ." He turns away. Mary is dazed. Mama is displeased. Surely Mr. Dickens cannot be mourning over some lost love *in front of his wife*?

But Mrs. Dickens says, "It was my younger sister, Mary. She died very suddenly, very young, exactly five years ago on 7th May – the day we were in Kingston."

"Bedtime," Mama says, very firmly. "Please excuse us, Kate. . . ." Dorothy and William say goodnight to Mrs. Dickens and follow Mama, who is speaking to Papa in the hall.

"Weeping about some dead girl in public!" says the major. "How delightful for Mrs. D. Does he fall into a fit every time he meets a girl called Mary?"

In which Mr. Dickens makes his intentions clear. Major Perry prepares for the worst:

Later, when everyone thinks they are asleep, Dorothy calls out to William and they creep down to eavesdrop on the dinner party through the banisters. Mr. Dickens seems to have cheered up again.

"When shall we begin rehearsals?" asks Miss Jane Ermatinger.

"On Monday, at noon," replies Mr. Dickens. "Word goes out; every day between noon and three o'clock until 24th May. I shall be the sternest taskmaster, Miss Jane. Wackford Squeers will be as the turtledove beside Charles Dickens, stage manager."

"You will act in the plays as well, I believe," Mama is saying. "We dared not look for that honor when we discussed the pieces."

"Indeed I shall; Mr. Snobbington, Alfred Highflyer, and, I think, Gallop, in *Deaf as a Post,* a mere couple of lines."

Dorothy has read the plays. Mr. Dickens has grabbed the best parts in two of them and now he is trying to sound modest by claiming that the third role is only a couple of lines. But they were Hugh's lines, Dorothy thinks.

"I believe you are appearing in *Deaf as a Post,* Mrs. Perry?" Mr. Dickens again.

"Yes, indeed." Dorothy can tell by her voice that Mama is very sorry that she agreed to do any such thing. It seems that anyone who is appearing in any of the plays is expected to be present in the theatre at all times, whether onstage or not.

"I pray nightly that there will be no riots, or wars, before the end of the month," Major Perry announces at breakfast. "If there are, then we stare defeat in the face. Half of the regiment is cantering about in the Theatre Royal with the superintendent of police."

In which Mr. Dickens turns out to be a man of many talents. Not everyone appreciates them:

Lieutenant Lincoln arrives daily at half past eleven, to escort Mama to the theatre.

"Is Mr. Dickens really like Wackford Squeers?" asks Dorothy, who knows all about the wicked schoolmaster from reading *Nicholas Nickleby.*

"Worse," says Hugh gloomily. "The only reason he doesn't knock us about is he's too short. He is actor, director, stage manager, carpenter, painter, and gas fitter, in ten places at once and shouting all the time. When his voice gives out, he pins up notices all over the back stage. *And* he's rewriting the plays as he goes."

"Isn't he just," grumbles Lieutenant Methuen, who has arrived with Hugh. "Every time I think I've got my lines off pat, he gives me a new set to learn and then calls me every kind of an idiot for not knowing them at once. And he keeps us awake till all hours at the hotel, playing the accordion. 'Home Sweet Home,' night after night, loud enough to raise the dead and never the same note twice."

In which Mrs. Darcy is discovered to be in an interesting condition, and Mr. Dickens reveals yet another accomplishment:

When Mama comes home again, Mrs. Dickens is with her. Mrs. Dickens was not at rehearsal, but had ventured out shopping with her maid and had a small mishap with a barrow in the street.

"Is the pain very bad?" Mama asks, seeing that Mrs. Dickens looks ready to weep. "Mary, fetch Cologne-water, and arnica, and a bandage."

"Oh, it isn't that, I am always falling down, I cannot seem to put my mind to anything, and we are both quite mad with homesickness – not that we aren't enjoying ourselves uncommonly here – everyone is so kind, but – but –"

"But what, dear Kate?" Mama swoops with a handkerchief to stanch the tears that are starting to fall. "Come now, tell me your trouble."

"No letters," Kate sobs. "No letters since Buffalo, in *April.* Not a word of my darlings – oh, I cannot endure it a moment longer."

Mr. Dickens does not seem mad with homesickness when he comes to collect his wife. Perhaps his purple coat and sky-blue vest keep his spirits up.

"Upon my word, Kate," he says, bounding into the garden where they are all taking tea with Mme Arnoux and Henriette. "I've a capital notion to fill your days *and* your mind, until we leave. Mrs. Darcy, who is to play Amy Templeton in *Deaf as a Post,* has discovered that she is to become a mother after Christmas and feels that she cannot continue in the part and –"

"Oh, the *poor* thing," cries Kate. Mr. Dickens, cut short, looks insulted.

"It seems to me that any woman who loved her husband would wish to be in the same happy condition as Mrs. Darcy," he says, stiffly.

"Oh, yes, of course," says Mrs. Dickens, on the verge of tears again. "But only think how she must be feeling."

"Dorothy, I think you might be excused," says Mama, exchanging glances with Mme Arnoux. "Take Henriette to see the new kittens."

Dorothy escorts Henriette to an arbor where William is lurking with the kittens in a basket – well in earshot.

"She doesn't want us to hear about Mrs. Darcy," he tells Henriette, "but she needn't worry. We watched the kittens come out. I think it is the same for babies."

"What I intended to say," Mr. Dickens continues, "was that since the part of Amy Templeton is now vacant, it occurred to me that you might take it, Kate."

"I act? On a stage?" Kate is thrown into a panic. "Oh no, indeed, I could never do it!"

"Oh, but you shall, my dear. You'll be the hit of the evening; I'll see to that."

"I beg you not to think of any such thing. I should do it so very badly, and everyone else will do it so well."

"I can assure you that, at present, no one is doing anything well," says her husband, "saving your presence, Mrs. Perry. But they will," he adds, "they will, if I have to magnetize them. Why, there's a thought,

Kate. Do you recollect how I magnetized *you* in Pittsburgh? Mrs. Perry, I made her weep. I made her laugh. I made her sleep. Kate, this time I shall make you act."

Dorothy peers through the branches and sees Mr. Dickens prance away to inspect a Grecian urn at the edge of the terrace. She beckons to the others and they walk sedately back to the tea party, as if they just happen to be passing.

"Have courage, Kate," Mama whispers to Mrs. Dickens, "I play Sophy Walton and we are always onstage together. Besides, we've scarcely forty lines between us."

In which Mr. Dickens takes an interest in interior design:

Meanwhile Mr. Dickens has wandered indoors and is prowling about, paying very particular attention to the parlor fire irons, the footstools, and the coal scuttle. He fingers the drapes. Mrs. Perry watches him nervously through the window.

"It's the color," Kate Dickens explains. "A most beautiful green, quite natural, like gooseberries. At home, in Devonshire Place, he has had the front door and the railings painted a very bright green."

Parrots, thinks Dorothy, picturing Mr. Dickens on a perch behind very bright green bars.

When the visitors have left, William sidles up to his mother. "Mama, we have something to ask you." Mrs. Perry looks alarmed.

"Oh, it's not about Mrs. Darcy," Dorothy says quickly. "We know all about that." Mrs. Perry looks even more alarmed. "But, Mama, how will Mr. Dickens *magnetize* Mrs. Dickens?"

"It is what they call Mesmerism," says Mrs. Perry. "A new science in which persons are made to do things they might not otherwise wish to do."

In which Mr. Dickens describes a sad loss to the professional stage:

A day or two later Mr. Dickens appears again while Mama is out. He is gallant to Mary, who seizes Dorothy by the hand the moment he appears and refuses to let go until he leaves, but he really seems to have come to visit the furniture. They watch him as he measures the drapes and calculates the width of Mama's cherry-wood console table. Jane Ermatinger told Mary only yesterday that her mother found him sizing up a tent-bed in the guest room.

"Believe it or not," says Mr. Dickens, "I very nearly became an actor." They can believe it. "I once wrote to the manager of the Covent Garden Theatre and was granted an interview. I practiced feverishly, but when the day came, I had the most terrible cold and pains in the face. I could not stir outdoors."

"Oh, for shame," says Mary. "And wouldn't they let you try again?"

"By the time I would have been ready to try again, Miss Perry, I was already earning a living as a writer. Wasn't that bad cold a stroke of good luck?"

"But you could still be an actor if you wanted," says Dorothy.

"Not at all," says Mr. Dickens. "I act only for charity, these days."

"But don't you do it because you like it?" Dorothy says, and Mary gives her arm an awful nip.

In which Mr. Dickens borrows a few items of furniture:

Next day they discover what Mr. Dickens has been planning. Hugh and Captain Granville arrive with a long, handwritten list.

"That looks like Mr. Dickens's writing," Mama says, suspiciously.

"I think everyone in the Garrison Amateurs knows that writing," says Captain Granville, bitterly. "There's not an inch of wall space backstage that isn't papered with Mr. Dickens's lists."

Mrs. Perry, scanning the list, feels she ought to have known what was coming.

"You want the coal scuttle –"

"Not I, Mrs. Perry," Hugh says, hurriedly. "Mr. Dickens."

"Mr. Dickens wishes me to favor him with the loan of the coal scuttle, the fire irons, the parlor drapes, a rustic seat, a Grecian urn, and my console table?"

"All stage properties are being borrowed from private houses," Captain Granville explains. "We have delivered similar lists to Mrs. Torrens and the Ermatingers. Mrs. Ermatinger is lending a whole bed."

"Good grief!" bellows Major Perry, returning to find the drapes coming down. "Now he intends to strip my house like a bailiff. Where will this end? Does he propose to borrow my boots?"

In which an invitation is sent out. Major Perry becomes more irritable than usual:

Next comes the gilt-edged card drafted by Mr. Dickens himself:

PRIVATE THEATRICALS COMMITTEE

Mrs. Torrens | *Mrs. Perry*
Wm. Ermatinger, Esq. | *Captain Torrens*
The Earl of Mulgrave

The Committee request the pleasure of MAJOR PERRY *and* MISS PERRY *at the Queen's Theatre, Montreal, on Wednesday evening, the twenty-fifth of May, at half-past Seven o'Clock precisely. It is to be expressly understood that this is a card of invitation and is therefore not transferable. To observe a strict observance of this understanding, it will be required to be presented at the door.*

The major erupts. "Ha! Does the fellow think I'm going to sell it to some passing fur-trader and pocket the profits? And what's this? Queen's Theatre? Where? Why? What's wrong with its real name?"

"It's in honor of Her Majesty, I believe," says Mrs. Perry. "Her birthday falls upon the eve of the performance."

"Birthday – fiddlesticks," retorts the major. "I suppose rather it's to prevent the general public from demanding the right to attend."

"Well, it will go back to being the Theatre Royal immediately afterwards," Mama soothes him. "On the 28th the pieces will be done again, in public."

The major turns puce. "In public? My wife, acting in public?"

"No, John, no. We ladies will be replaced by professional actresses from Mr. Latham's regular company. Our modesty will be preserved."

"A damn raree-show, the whole thing," the major snarls. But he accepts the invitation – for Mary's sake, naturally.

In which Queen Victoria celebrates her 23rd birthday:

Dorothy and William have not been invited to the theatre, so as a consolation Mama arranges for them to see the troops parade and fire a *feu de joie* in honor of Queen Victoria's birthday, which falls on the day of the dress rehearsal. When Mlle Fleurie brings them home again at teatime, Mama has not returned and Papa is striding about the house and threatening to shoot Mr. Dickens. Mlle Fleurie is also in a vile temper. Dorothy overhears her telling Amalie, the parlor maid, how she resents having to spend the afternoon watching the army of occupation firing salutes for a foreign queen. Dorothy wonders whether to tell Mama about this. All the servants are French; are they planning a rebellion of their own? But then she considers: Mama, too, is French Canadian. She decides on balance that Mlle Fleurie is probably suffering from nothing worse than sore feet. She has been standing all afternoon in new shoes. And Amalie watched the parade, too.

VR
VR

In which the dress rehearsal does not go as well as it might. No lives are lost, however:

Mama returns at midnight and does not come down to breakfast. It is not until midday that the household hears about the dress rehearsal: how the scenery collapsed; how stage properties, including the coal scuttle, vanished; how Captain Granville fell out of a window and blacked his eye; how the real coal fire, which burns in a grate during *Past Two in the Morning,* spat flame and set light to Mrs. Torrens's tablecloth; how Mr. Dickens shouted at Captain Willoughby and Captain Willoughby offered to run him through with his cavalry sword; how Mr. Dickens shouted at Jane Ermatinger and sent her into hysterics; how Mr. Dickens laughed when Dr. Griffen choked on a chicken bone in *Deaf as a Post* and Dr. Griffen tried to poke him in the eye.

"Oh, I cannot face the performance tonight," Mama moans feebly. "How am I to get out of it, John?"

"Take a hint from Mrs. Dickens and break your neck?" suggests the major.

In which the performance goes well and Lieutenant Lincoln's prospects look rosier than they usually do:

But all is well on the night. Dorothy and William are in bed when the theatre party returns, but they steal downstairs to hear how the Queen's Theatre was filled to the doors – six hundred people in the house. The commander in chief was there, and the governor-general, come down especially from Kingston. The band of the 23rd Royal Welsh Fusiliers played in the intervals, and no one forgot their words, or injured themselves, or murdered Mr. Dickens.

Happiest of all, it seems, was Kate Dickens, playing as if possessed, or magnetized, but in fact only transformed by joy and relief, for not two hours before the play began, Lord Mulgrave galloped up to Rasco's Hotel in person, waving a budget of letters just delivered from the steam packet. Mrs. Dickens was so overcome that she set fire to her front hair with a candle.

"And so that's an end to playacting," says Papa, who has enjoyed himself, but does not intend to admit it. "When may we have our furniture back?"

"Not quite yet," says Mama. "Mr. Dickens and Kate are going down to Quebec for a day or two with Lord Mulgrave, but they'll be back for the public performance on Saturday. Then they are off to Laprairie for a few days more in America. And after that, home to England."

"Where the confounded creature will no doubt write an insulting book about North America," Papa says, and goes in search of a stiff

brandy to help him recover from having had such a good time.

"I'll tell you one thing," says Mama to Mary, as they go upstairs, "fame or no fame, I had sooner be Mrs. John Perry, my love, than Mrs. Charles Dickens."

"Oh, so would I!" Mary cries. "That is, I mean, I should rather be Mrs. Hugh Lincoln than Mrs. Charles Dickens."

Dorothy, loitering on the landing, says to William, "We had better tell that to Hugh tomorrow, so he can propose before she changes her mind."

In which Lieutenant Lincoln buys a parrot. It looks strangely familiar:

Next morning Hugh arrives with a present for Mary. A seaman on Water Street has sold him a parrot that can sing in Spanish and pray like a Christian, so the seaman says. It can also swear like a trooper, but this was not mentioned. It is a small and dazzling bird – vivid green, red-beaked, and bright of eye.

"What shall you call him?" says Hugh. The Perrys look at each other and Dorothy wonders who is going to speak first.

THE END